Corie

Universe

Feeder

Walter Eckland

*****

ALSO BY WALTER ECKLAND
Corie Castle Builder (Corie Universe Feeder Book Two)
Corie World Creator (Corie Universe Feeder Book Three)

*****

<u>One Green Fermented Chapter</u>

A Pickle Sandwich
or
the Pickle Sandwich
or
one Pickle Sandwich
or
THE PICKLE SANDWICH!
Whichever you choose, all I know is that it started with a/one/the/THE Pickle Sandwich.

And a fish.

Two: The Beginning(s)

Corie: tall, thin, scruffy, female, student, blondish, smart, creative, outspoken, trouble-finding, precocious (whatever THAT means), eager, mature, silly, immature, messy-roomed, imaginative, animal-loving girl.

Corie lives in a suburb of a big city in the Northeast. Want to know which city? Well, I can't tell you that.

The house she lives in:

- is painted white;
- has many rooms including, two and a half bathrooms (Corie still wonders where the other half went);
- has a big, big, big, huge front yard;
- has an even bigger, bigger, bigger, more huge back yard;
- is old;
- contains two irritating older but not more mature brothers;
- has the neatest boy-you-can-get-messy-and-in-big-trouble-after-playing-in-it-and-going-into-the-house-and-lying-upside-down-all-muddy-on-your-bed-to-read-a-book-even-though-reading-is-good-for-you stream next to it;
- has plenty of food;

- contains one dog (although, it is often asked, "Why we can't have fifteen dogs? That's silly. I'll take care of them.");
- is happy;
- looks good in winter;
- has great snakes in the yard, but that's another story;
- has a fox who visits the yard;
- is also visited by white-tailed deer, as well as one weird deer with no tail and a goofy limp who eats mushrooms and doesn't run away when you go outside and look at him;
- and contains a mother and a father.

That snake story is pretty interesting, and I wish I could tell you more about the trouble that whole thing caused but I can't right now.

Anyhow, anyhoo, anywhatever...

Whenever I get off track and try to tell you something else or go off and tell another story—like the time Smelly Timmy, too young to sled, went down the "world's most incredible slippery, slidey, sled run in Corie's back yard that only costs a quarter to use all day" and broke his wrist and lost a tooth, and Corie got mad because she never got her quarter but got in more trouble than he did, even though he welched—whenever I get off track like that and I remember what I was supposed to be doing, I end up saying, "Anyhow, or anyhoo, or anywhatever," and then try to get back to the story.

I think.

Anysomething.

It's a nice house in a nice neighborhood with nice parents and irritating brothers and Corie.

And a pickle and a fish.

Two: The Beginning(s) Some More

The pickle.

Listen. Dad, who is not so, so bad as dads go, actually likes pickles. He was home making late lunch, or maybe early dinner, and Corie was Corie-ing around, not doing anything really, but kind of doing it wrong anyway. Dad was making lunch/dinner, and Corie said for the ten-thousandth time, "What's to eat?"

Dad finally said, "Pickle sandwiches," even though Corie hates (or as Mom says, "dislikes immensely") pickles.

The pickle in question:

- was green—and not a nice shade of green like the green stuff that came out the time Corie threw up all over the bedroom after the birthday party thingy happened;
- was wrinkled (aren't they all?);
- smelled;
- was some new kind that was even bigger than the old kind;
- came from a jar;
- was cold;
- and wouldn't be eaten by the dog who ate ASOLUTELY ANYTHING (Corie knew this because she had tried

feeding the dog ABSOLUTELY
ANYTHING).

I'm not going to tell you the name of Corie's dog. She thinks if you know the name of her dog and what a great pull-you-in-the-sled, chase-you-through-the-house-and-the-muddy-stream, and eat-the-vegetables-you-pass-her-under-the-table-except-for-pickles dog she is, you'll come to the Northeast and steal her.

That's why I can't tell you the name of Corie's dog and have to just call her "Corie's dog," because you might steal her.

Corie's brothers' names are Robert and James.

<u>Two: The Beginning(s) Still More</u>

The fish in question...

...was served at the early dinner/late lunch on last night's rice, reheated in the micro-wavy.

At least there were no leftover green beans.

The fish wasn't that bad, but you never want to admit to your parents that you like fish, or else you'll get it all the time instead of good dinner stuff like popcorn, pudding, and Popsicles.

Anyhoo.

Dad suggested she eat his extra half of a pickle sandwich and all of the fish, but Corie was way, way, way too full from all that rice, thank you very much.

Brothers Robert/Bobby and James/James came in around then, but they had more important stuff to do like go up to their room and talk about baseball or pick their noses.

If you ask them about the hockey game they're watching on TV when it's in the middle of baseball season and it's clearly a baseball game they're watching, it's guaranteed to earn you a bop on the arm; and if you fall down or bump into the wall like the bop really hurts or something, then maybe the brother gets in big or medium trouble and can't watch baseball for like a month or two years or until there's enough money in his savings account to pay for college.

Dad said to Corie, "There are people starving all over the world and right here in our very own town, and boy, it would be a shame to waste food, even if it is pickles and fish," so that's how all this started.

"Well, Dad, I couldn't agree more." (They hate it or at least immensely dislike it when you agree with them.) "Dad, it truly, truly, deeply would be a shame to waste a perfectly good pickle half and a hunk of fish that could be used to feed all the starving people in our town, or at least the known universe."

"But—and I mean, BUT—wouldn't it be better if we could put this itty, bitty piece of fish and pickle to better use and feed many more people and kids and goats? Wouldn't it? Wouldn't it?"

"Anyhow, what I thought was we (you and me and that new shovel I'm not supposed to use because I broke the last one, even though, who would know that a shovel would break if you just accidentally dropped it from the second-floor bedroom window while trying to get a crow off the roof? And no, I did not almost fall out the window with the shovel, since my pants were caught on the bed anyway)...anyhow, couldn't we just use that new shovel and me and you to plant the piece of fish and the pickle in the front yard and grow a pickle-and-fish tree to feed more people? Couldn't we? It would grow lots of pickles and fish, and some people like pickles and fish, so we could feed lots of people instead of just one girl who's pretty full from all that rice anyway."

"I never get to do anything fun."

You would expect Dad to give a long, speechless look, like there's a piece of gum stuck in your hair that's so long it trails down to your feet and gets caught in the carpet and has twenty colors and maybe marshmallows in it. You'd expect him to say, "I wonder whose child you are anyway and if there REALLY WAS some kind of a mistake between the hospital and the zoo that day, or at least the circus."

But instead, Dad said, "Sure. Go ahead. Please use the new shovel. Plant the fish and pickle and feed many, many more people in the world. That's a great idea, and I know you can do it."

The End of the Beginning(s): Five

Which takes half the fun—or at least a third of the fun, or maybe eleven-sixteenths of the fun—out of it, but so what? We're talking:
digging,
    watering,
        planting,
            out-siding,
                new shoveling and
                    mess-making
                (approved even!) and
Corie doesn't have to eat the pickle or fish, which has to be pretty cold and gross now 'cause it came out of the micro-wavy around ten hours ago.
    Pretty good for a Thursday.
    That's how this all began.

Part 2, Chapter 1, or Chapter 6 if you want, even though there were three Chapter 2s in that last part

Anything worth doing is worth doing with lots more tools, equipment, friends, mud, time, books, enthusiasm, trouble, and more tools.

Corie went out in the front yard to plant.

Corie is not capable of walking to the first likely spot in the yard and planting.

Oh no.

Oh no.

OH NO.

Corie must walk around and a-square and front-wards and backwards and other kinds of - wards and up and down and crawl and skip all over the front yard, until the exact correct, right, perfect, never-been-better, of-course-this-is-the-one-and-only-absolutely-perfect-place-for-it spot is found.

Or at least until no less than four neighborhood children have come over to see what's going on and to help, which they can only do if they do EXACTLY what Corie tells them to do, EXACTLY as Corie tells them and EXACTLY when Corie tells them, or else they won't get to help next time, but they will get to help this time, so that next time when they're not helping, they'll remember how much fun it is to help.

But even before the walking-around-the-yard stuff happened, the research part had to happen. You always need to research stuff before you do it.

Corie has the biggest and best collection of books on every subject in the whole world. In addition to having her own books, she is the number one visitor to the suburb-town-that-I won't-name public library.

You would think the librarians would appreciate her coming there since she is there more than anyone else in the whole town, but the folks at the public library don't seem to particularly appreciate her at all.

If you were a librarian and you had to look at the SAME books all day, wouldn't you want a girl coming in, always asking for books you have to order from the big library in the other town? Especially if those books are about important things likes snakes or space or London or waste water treatment plants or traffic signals from around the world or planting or hot air balloons or white-tailed deer without tails or more snakes?

Well? If you were a librarian, wouldn't you want Corie around your library? If you are a librarian and do want her around, please call or write and tell her, but don't e-mail her because she isn't allowed to use e-mail for a long, long time.

Even though the e-mail thing wasn't really her fault.

Sort of.

There was no time to go to the library to research this one. That pickle and fish needed planting, and it was already late, late afternoon, maybe even early, early evening.

The research stuff had to be done with Corie's own books in her own library where you can be as noisy as you like and don't get the "SHHHH!" all the time, except when it's two or three in the morning and you say, "I just had to look that up right away, and when I found the answer, of course I screamed, 'OH YEAH!' Wouldn't you? Well, you are awake now, so let me tell you all about it!"

Anyhow, anyhoo.

Research accomplished, facts learned, concepts conceptualized, plans planned, and ready to plant.

The perfect spot, in the perfect yard, in the perfect neighborhood with the almost-close-to-someday-maybe-perfect girl.

Now there were five helpers, and Smelly Timmy's arm was pretty good by then, so he might, just might, be able to use the shovel.

Fortunately, there was a can of orangey-red or maybe reddy-orange spray paint in the garage so the construction site could be properly and officially marked. It would have been oh so helpful to spray big numbers on the helpers' backs like she wanted to. Unfortunately, you know how helpers can be with simple and practical suggestions like that.

The hole began to grow.

And the dirt from the hole went in the wheelbarrow.

And the wheelbarrow dirt was dumped in the back yard.

Now there was a good-sized hole and only one banged worker foot, which wasn't bad for a job this size.

There is only one proper way to plant something like this. Only the person who had done the research would possibly know what the proper way is.

The pickle and fish cannot possibly be put in the hole all alone! They'll never grow into a pickle-and-fish tree that way. Just the right ingredients need to be added.

A little orangey-red spray paint is perfect, as is a penny, a leaf, a twig, the broken robin egg shell, the little "Inspected by #19" tag from Jenna's pocket, five pine needles, no pine cones, and some sand. The absolute best thing—and the most important—is the sticky, gooey, wet mud from the stream.

If you think back on this later, after you hear all about what happened, maybe you'll think the stream mud was the magic in all of this and what started things going the way they did.

Maybe it was the mud. But then again, maybe it was radioactive snot from Smelly Timmy.

Finally, you're ready to place the pickle and the fish in the hole, and of course they don't get broken into little pieces. They get placed on the mud with the small fish on the bottom and the smaller pickle on top of the fish.

Mud—more mud, wetter mud, smellier mud—gently placed on the pickle and the fish.

Then back to the back yard to load up the wheelbarrow with the dirt that was taken out earlier. No, it would not have been just as easy to leave the dirt in the wheelbarrow. It had to be dumped in the back yard. Then it had to be reloaded into the wheelbarrow and wheeled to the front yard. That was what the plan called for.

Add the dirt to the top and pat it down with the new shovel, and then the second-best after-the-mud part: watering.

NO HELPERS NEED APPLY for the watering part.

The pickle and the fish and the mud and the proper stuff watered, just the right amount.

The label on the piece of wood that came from that weird thing in the garage was added with a sign that said:

CAUTION
Pickle-and-Fish Tree
Growing Here Soon

Seven

Just about everyone in the world says Corie has no patience. They are wrong.

With things that deserve patience, Corie has it to spare.

Growing pickle-and-fish trees deserve patience, as well as water and sun and care and attention.

Homework and church and aunts and hair-cutting and dishwashing and putting things away and librarians do not deserve or need patience.

Every day, Corie watered her tree and patiently waited.

Eight

There's a guy who lives up the road who has a dog. He walks that dog late at night and early in the morning. Corie's dad walks her dog (no name) late at night and early in the morning and meets up with the weirdest and nicest people. Sometimes he meets up with that guy up the street who owns a restaurant in town. That guy works in his restaurant most of the day and pays kids to walk his dog and play with it in the middle of the day, and he has no wife.

He met up with Dad one night or early morning and asked about the sign. Dad told him Corie was growing a pickle-and-fish tree and was going to feed many, many people in the world.

The next day, they saw him at his restaurant, and he said that when her pickles and fish started to grow, he'd put them on the menu. He was quite, quite serious. Her brothers just sat there with their mouths open like they were trying to eat something even though no food—not even the rolls—had come yet.

Corie told him, "I'd love to, but I'm trying to feed the people in the world who have no food, but thank you very much. Maybe if there's any extra, I can give you some."

Twenty days, thirteen hours, twenty-six minutes, and who-cares-how-many seconds later, Corie's tree began to grow. On a Thursday.

Every day she continued to water it, and it grew even more.

Except when it rained. Then it was watered, but not by Corie.

The only day it wasn't watered by Corie or the rain was the day she went to a birthday sleepover and begged, "Dad, please, please, please don't forget to water my tree, or I'll walk home from the sleepover and do it myself, and you'll be out walking the dog anyway, so don't forget. I'll put a note on the leash and call you too."

Every day it was watered, and it grew.

It was planted properly, watered properly, and it grew very improperly. It grew improperly quickly.

In a week it was 18 inches or 1½ feet or 1/2 yard or .4572 meters tall. In two weeks it was 29.5 inches tall. How many meters is that? Look it up or go bother your local librarian about it. They love it when you bother them about books about measurements. Really, they do.

Ten. Other Things Are Growing Too/Also

The guy who walks his dog late at night and early in the morning, has no wife, and owns a restaurant always puts ads in the local newspaper. Why he does that is a mystery since nobody from out of town ever reads the small suburb paper, and everyone in town knows about the restaurant already anyway because it's been there since the time of the dinosaurs, and it has a huge, big sign.

Anyway, the dog/no wife/restaurant guy places ads in the paper all the time. When he places the ads, he talks to the newspaper owner. Maybe he talks about the weather or the ad or hockey versus baseball or his favorite color or tonight's restaurant special or dogs or Saturn and its twenty-three or maybe twenty-four moons. One day, he talks about the wonderful growing pickle-and-fish tree he sees when he takes his daily/nightly dog walks.

The newspaper owner listens. He's supposed to do that, kind of like the guidance lady at school who is SUPPOSED to listen but likes to interrupt and shake her head and ask the same questions week after week, sometimes day after day or whenever you get sent to see her.

The newspaper guy listened.

A few days, or maybe 1.7328 weeks later, he was driving around chasing after the fire engine to see if he could get a picture of a house or a car or nuclear power plant burning so he could put it on the cover of his paper, and maybe then somebody from out of town would read it.

But there was no fire and no water and no hoses and no burning and no picture that day. I guess the fire people just felt like driving around in circles. There were loud siren circles, but no fire.

What there was, however, was a sign next to a little tree that said:

CAUTION
Pickle-and-Fish Tree
Growing Here ~~Soon~~
NOW

The newspaper guy who listens took a picture of the sign and the tree.

He put the picture on the cover of the weekly paper the very next Thursday instead of the fire picture he didn't get because there was no fire.

The adults in the town looked at the picture of the pickle-and-fish tree instead of the picture of the fire since there wasn't one to look at.

The kids in the town looked at the picture of the pickle-and-fish tree.

The kids in the town made the parents in the town drive them over to Corie's to see (but not touch) the pickle-and-fish tree.

The parents in the town did the guidance counselor head-shake thing and took their kids to see (but not touch) the pickle-and-fish tree.

Lots of the above happened.

The newspaper guy heard that lots of the people in town (but nobody from out of town) were reading his paper and going to see the pickle-and-fish tree.

The guy now knew what sells papers.

He didn't drive by and take another picture. Instead, he called and MADE AN APPOINTMENT with Corie to drive by and take another picture and maybe ask her and her dad and Smelly Timmy or anyone else a few questions to go with the picture, maybe even two pictures.

Before Thursday, which is when the weekly newspaper comes out.

Corie to Mother and Father (shut up, Robert and James):

"I'm certainly not wearing a dress for ANY news-picture guy."

"My room looks fine, and he's not going up to see it anyway."

"Why can't I …?"

"Why should I …?"

"That's not fair. It is MY pickle-and-fish tree."

"Yes, Mother, the rest of the kids in the neighborhood had to be told and invited over. After all, they helped and may be able to help on the next project. No, they're not just coming over to see me get interviewed."

"Yes I brushed my teeth and washed my face and hands."

"Well, there can be dirt under your fingernails after you wash your hands if you go outside and get some dirt after you wash your hands and then rub said dirt into your fingers because no news-picture guy is going to believe you planted a pickle-and-fish tree if you don't have dirt under your fingernails or at least on your forehead."

"Yes, I'm quite sure I know what inappropriate words are as well as personal subjects because you mention them just about every day. Why you keep mentioning them I can't imagine since they're inappropriate."

"Yes...No...Yes...No...Yes...No...Yes...No."

There are no Floor Thirteens in elevators except in old, old buildings, and who would ride in an elevator in an old, old building?

The news-picture guy was not that bad.

He was almost nice for an adult.

He came at eleven in the morning. He wore a tie. He drove a red, kind of dumpy old car. He had no dog. He went to the same college as Mom, but in a TOTALLY different year because not all adults are the same age. He was polite. He carried a small pad and a large pad and a camera and other camera junk in a bag.

The interview began.

The early dinner/late lunch was described.

The pickle sandwich was described.

The fish on re-micro-wavy-ed rice was described.

The shovel problem was discussed.

The offer to view the new shovel was declined.

The research was discussed, especially the part about having to use her own library because there wasn't time to get to the town library.

The helper friends were discussed, even the part about them not wanting numbers to be spray painted on their backs. The suggestion was made that maybe the news-picture guy could number his workers, and it would be easier to tell them what to do.

The proper planting instructions were discussed.

The ingredients for planting were discussed.

The stream mud was discussed in great detail.

The watering was discussed.

The absolutely amazing growth rate of the pickle-and-fish tree was discussed.

The interview ended.

Time for pictures. First, a nice picture or three of the home research library in Corie's room. Mom's eyes rolled out of her head and across the floor and bonked Corie on the head about then.

Seventeen more pictures of the home research library with Corie in some and not in some.

At least three rolls of pictures of the tree that is 7 feet, 9 ¾ inches tall.

Fourteen pictures of the stream and stream mud were taken, and it was said, "I'm sorry I knocked you in the stream, Mr. News-picture Guy, but at least the camera didn't fall in."

Fourteen

That very Thursday, Corie and her tree and her friends and her stream mud pictures were all on the cover of the local paper with an article about them with 376 words, not counting periods or commas because they're not even words.

That week, more kids in the town made the parents in the town drive them over to Corie's to see (but not touch) the pickle-and-fish tree.

Even some people who weren't parents and didn't have kids came to see the pickle-and-fish tree.

Every day, it was watered, and it grew and grew quickly.

Fifteen

Corie's parents are always saying she is highly intelligent and imaginative. They ruin that by also saying if she applied herself to something constructive, they would be amazed.

Corie amazed her parents right then and there.

Here's what she did:

Remember how the pickle and fish were planted so they could feed all of the starving people in the town, or at least the known universe? Well, do you?

Another way you can feed all the people in the town and the country and the world besides giving them pickles and fish is if you give them some money to buy food. Popcorn, pudding, and Popsicles cost money, you know.

What Corie did was to put out a large empty water bottle—and by large, I mean a big one, the kind that gurgle when you use them in the water machine thing and you end up almost peeing on the floor because you drink so much water just to make the thing gurgle.

Corie put out a large empty water bottle next to the pickle-and-fish tree with a small, tastefully done sign about voluntary contributions to help feed people until such time as pickles and fish were readily available.

Of course it was tastefully done: Mom absolutely, no chance, not in her yard, nuh-uh would let her put up the first sign she made, which was as big as a small elephant if the small elephant ate three school buses. (Of course, that wouldn't be a bad idea, because then they couldn't bus kids to school, so they would have to cancel. Elephant-ate-the-buses days would be even better than snow days.)

The sign said:

PLEASE ENJOY LOOKING AT (BUT DON'T TOUCH) THE PICKLE-AND-FISH TREE AND IF YOU WANT TO HELP PEOPLE WHO ARE STARVING TODAY THAT CAN'T WAIT FOR THE PICKLES AND FISH TO GROW PLEASE DONATE MONEY INTO THE JAR.

Corie took all of her savings and put it in the bottle in the yard next to the tasteful sign: $12.74.

Do you know why she put all of her savings in the bottle?

Because Dad said once that it takes money to make money.

If you take $12.74, that should make more money.

16 Corie's Parents Talk to Each Other

One night when Corie was asleep, her parents had a lengthy but quiet conversation. They wondered what was going on with the tree. They wondered why it was growing so quickly. They puzzled over the concept of the tasteful sign and the donating of the $12.74.

They didn't disagree with the sign or the twelve scoots. Mom got kind of teary eyed and talked about Corie maybe really actually growing up.

They talked some more about the tree and the watering and the fast growing.

There are 5,718 books on the third floor of the town library, or at least there were two years ago on Saturday, July 17, when Corie counted each and every one.

You would think a librarian would be interested in knowing that riveting, fascinating, and helpful fact. Well, they're not—not even the head librarian.

Anywhatever.

Mom and Dad talked a lot. Mom and Dad worried a lot. Mom and Dad shook their heads a lot, then and for weeks and weeks to come.

Dad got up and went outside to walk the dog. He looked at the tree and the contribution bottle and the sign.

Later, Mom got even more (happy?) teary eyed and went to sleep.

Parents!

The news-picture guy just about had a heart attack. Some lady from two towns over who owns another newspaper called him because people in her town were not buying her paper but were buying his Corie picture paper instead. Lots of them.

The news-picture guy listened. He was good at that.

That night, the news-picture guy had dinner at the dog walk/no wife guy's restaurant. He had the chicken pot pie. His mouth was open even before the rolls came too.

That Thursday, the news-picture guy changed the layout of the front of his newspaper, which he hadn't done in about 100 years, or at least since he took over from his father.

He made a place on the front of the paper where every week there would be a new picture of the pickle-and-fish tree.

He even had two stories inside: one was about the tree, and the other was about the contribution bottle. He himself had donated the last time he took a picture and did not get knocked into the stream.

Public and Private Charities, by Julien Dellaporta, 1992, Page 53 explains all about how to set up a charitable bank account. Corie let the bank manager borrow her copy of that book when she set up the charity account at his bank, and he, himself, donated to her jar.

The news-picture guy put this in his next paper:

Donations may be made in the bottle at the tree...

OR

Mailed to:

Bank Seven

Charitable Gift Account

Pickle-and-Fish Tree Donations

P.O. Box 341

Corie's Town

Corie's Northeast State

Corie's Quite Zippy, Zip Code

One time a dopey bird flew right into the window of the family room while everyone was there. They all went out and looked at it. It looked dead. Robert and James wanted to poke it with a stick, but Dad wouldn't let them. Dad made everyone go inside. If the bird was not dead, then it would get up and fly away on its own. The bird was not dead, but it did not get up and fly away on its own. It crawled over near the garage door and got snowed on.

In the middle of the night, if you leaned out of Corie's window just right with a flashlight and binoculars, you could see the bird out by the garage getting snowed on.

Corie went out and got that bird. She put her (or him—who can tell?) in a box. She put the box in the back hall and closed the door. She went back to sleep.

Apparently, the bird could fly.

That was found out in the morning when Mom went into the back hall to get the stuff that was going to the dry cleaners on her way to work.

It was covered with bird doo.

It was not a pretty site/sight.

Neither was Corie, standing in the back hall in her PJs with a major bed-head thing going on.

I won't repeat the first ten minutes of discussion. (Isn't a discussion when two people talk back and forth? Well, there was some forth, but no back.)

More at the eleventh minute:

"But they're going to the cleaners anyway!"

"Aren't cleaners supposed to clean stuff?"

"That's impossible! The clothes are black, and the bird poop is white. Do you think they won't be able to find it?"

"What attitude?"

"But if they're cleaners, why can't they clean things?"

"They're the best cleaners."

"Because their sign says BEST CLEANERS, that's why."

"What?"

"Who?"

"When?"

"Yes, I fed the bird, and I don't know what time it was, but it was way too late to be looking at the clock."

Am I off track again?

Oh.

Anyhoo. Anywhatever...

Every day donations were made in the gurgle jar and at the bank. Pennies and nickels and dimes and quarters and occasionally a dollar were put in the gurgle jar.

The librarian school must have a whole semester of classes on how not to be very happy and how to never, ever smile. Some librarians must get straight-A grades in that class, but luckily, lots of them must skip it, or maybe for some of them there was an elephant-ate-the-buses day that kept them from learning how to look so un-smiley. When you come in the door of the library, there are three major things:

1..A big desk where you check out books.

2..The office of the head librarian, which has a big glass window in it.

3..Across from the head librarian's office is a rack with the current newspapers from the big Northeast city, as well as a little rack for the local town comes-out-on-Thursday paper.

Every minute of every day when she wasn't in the bathroom or downstairs eating yogurt, the head librarian had to look at a picture of the pickle-and-fish tree through the window of her office.

Corie's pickle-and-fish tree.

Corie, library trouble-causing, book-requesting, noisy girl.

The head librarian could have taught that class about not smiling. I guess she could have taught the frowning class too.

I do like the number nineteen but there is no chapter nineteen. It happens.

<u>tWeNtY</u>

It had been seven Thursdays since the first sprout of the pickle-and-fish tree. The tree was twenty-one feet tall and had improper leaves growing on it. They were improper because there were two kinds of them—on the same tree.

One kind was sort of round and dark green and shiny. Another kind was sort of long and thin and light green and not shiny and smelled nice. The two kinds of leaves were on the same branches. Some branches had more shiny leaves, and some branches had more not-shiny leaves, but all of the branches had leaves.

Every day it was watered, and it grew. Sometimes it grew up. Sometimes it grew out and sideways.

Every Thursday, there was a picture of it in the paper.

One Tuesday, the news-picture guy went to the miserable, grumpy printer guy. He told him that he wanted 4,500 copies of his newspaper every Thursday from now on instead of the 2,550 he had gotten every week since about the dinosaurs. Grumpy printer guy grunted and asked, "Why? Nobody really moves into or out of town much, and nobody from out of town ever reads your paper."

The news-picture guy listened. He didn't really say anything except that he wanted 4,500 copies of his paper from then on.

The miserable, grumpy printer guy was still miserable and grumpy when he left.

You know the other news-picture lady in the town two towns over? She changed the front of her paper, too, and put the picture of the pickle-and-fish tree on the cover every week and the important stuff about the donations. She herself donated (a lot because she's got plenty of money and very nice shoes).

The kids in the town two towns over looked at the picture of the pickle-and-fish tree.

The kids in the town two towns over made the parents in the town two towns over drive them over to Corie's to see (but not touch) the pickle-and-fish tree.

Three weeks later, the news-picture lady in the town two towns over went to see the miserable, grumpy printer guy to ask him to print more copies of her paper every Thursday.

The miserable, grumpy printer guy was still miserable and grumpy when she left.

If you knew the name of the big Northeast city near where Corie lived, and if you thought about the names of the towns kind of north of the big city, which is where Corie's town is, most of those towns around there started printing pictures of the pickle-and-fish tree. They printed stuff about the donations too.

The miserable, grumpy printer guy was still miserable and grumpy after those news-picture owners asked for more papers every Thursday or Monday or Sunday or whenever they printed their paper, one of them even in color.

Every day, donations were made in the gurgle jar and at the bank. Pennies and nickels and dimes and quarters and more and more often dollars and sometimes five-dollar bills and ten-dollar bills were put in the gurgle jar.

Every day, the pickle-and-fish tree was watered, and it grew. Quite improperly.

Blackjack!

Do I really have to tell you what happened when the TV station from the big city sent a camera crew and a real reporter up to take pictures of Corie and her library and her friends and the shovel and the stream mud and the pickle-and-fish tree and the donation jars; there are five of them, and they fill up every week; sometimes they even have twenties in them, and once or twice or seven times, an actual FIFTY- OR HUNDRED-DOLLAR BILL!

Do I have to tell you about the bank manager guy being interviewed about all the money that comes to the pickle-and-fish tree fund and why he won't return Corie's book? After all, she is a LENDING library—not a GIVING library.

Do I have to tell you that the pictures of the stuff I mentioned above were shown on the news and were seen all over the state?

Do I have to tell you that the other TV stations sent their cameras and reporters, and one even sent a helicopter to take pictures too?

Do I have to tell you that every kid in town thought Corie was the absolute best in the world because she was on TV?

Did you know Corie almost never, ever even watches TV because it's much more fun to read?

If I did tell you about all that, would you be able to figure out on your own that lots and lots more kids from lots and lots of towns all over the state made their parents take them to see (but never touch, especially the two-different-kinds-of-leaves part) the pickle-and-fish tree?

Now, if lots of kids and parents and even more adults with no kids from all over the state came to your yard to look at a pickle-and-fish tree and put money of all kinds in the donation jars, would you have set up a lemonade and cookie stand in the other corner of your yard, not too close to the pickle-and-fish tree, where you and your friends and your friends' friends and their cousins—even the ones from Canada—could help sell lemonade and water and cookies and split the money evenly and put half the money in the Charity Feeding donation fund, and all of the kids made so much money that there will be enough to put in their college funds and even spend some on not-very-practical things at all?

Well? Do I really have to tell you that? I hope not. I'm sure you can figure it out on your own.

Corie did it, and so did her friends, and so did their friends, and so did their cousins—even the ones from Canada.

The restaurant/dog/no wife guy had to open his restaurant earlier and stay open later because he was so busy, but he still had time to meet a very nice lady who might someday be his wife. She really likes dogs.

Did you ever get a splinter in your thumb? Anyhoo. Anyhow. Anywhatever.

Feed 'em.

When you have five donation bottles that fill up every week and a charity bank account that fills up every day, there comes a time when you should use that money to feed people.

Corie and Corie alone got to decide how to spend that money, even though Dad got to comment a little.

(She had researched the charity money part really, really well in her own library and the town library and even on the Internet, but she swears she didn't use e-mail while she was logged in. I never told you about that research, but it still happened. I never told you the sun came up today, but that still happened too, at least where I live.)

Anythis, anythat.

There is one grocery store in Corie's town.

The one grocery store in Corie's town has a list of names.

The names on the list are all the people in the town who don't have enough money to buy the food they need every week. Know how Corie figured out whose name goes on the list? Research!

Every person whose name is on that list can go to the grocery store anytime and get not a 10 or 20 or 30 or 40 or 50 or 60 or 70 or 80 or 90 or

99 percent discount on food. No, the people on that list can get a 100 percent discount as long as they buy food and don't spend the discount on stupid things like cigarettes and lottery tickets. The people who don't have enough money to buy the food they need every week only have to pay 0 percent.

There is a place called the World Food Bank. They feed people in countries all over the world. They are based in Geneva, Switzerland. Corie has never been to Switzerland, but she would like to go there. She wonders if they really yodel there, and if they invented yogurt there because it sounds like yodel, or at least starts with the same letter or two.

Every two weeks, Corie had the Bank Seven in town send a check to the World Food Bank. Every day, the World Food Bank used Corie's donation money to buy and deliver food to almost every country in the world, even the ones whose name aren't on the map yet since they're brand new. Even brand new countries have people that don't have enough food.

Every day, people and kids and cousins and aunts came to see the pickle-and-fish tree and donate more money.

Did your tree house ever fall down or at least kind of tip over because it was built on the top of the hill where it's windy?

Someone ran a car wash once in their yard a few years ago. It was a great soapy, watery carwash. It didn't earn any money; in fact, it may even have lost a little. Learning is very important. Here are some things that were learned when someone ran a car wash in their yard a few years ago:

- Cloth seats inside cars do not get washed with soapy water and buckets and hoses.
- Spraying the hose at cars that don't stop at your carwash is bad, even more so if their windows are open.
- Police cars visit houses where water is sprayed at cars that don't stop at your car wash.
- Putting green food coloring in the water when you wash a car will not change the color of the car to green, no matter how much green food coloring you use, even if all of your friends go to their houses and get all their Mom's and Dad's green food coloring.
- Soapy water does not taste good.
- Your allowance gets seriously cut for a long time when your dad has to pay for somebody's cloth seats to get dried and fix the scratch that wasn't on their car roof before.
- Proper research is important before any project, even one that sounds like fun—like a soapy, watery carwash.
- Librarians don't get taught in librarian school how to order any more than five

books at a time from the big library in the other town, even if they are small books.

- Shaking their head seems to make adults feel better when normal things happen.

Anyhoo.

23. bot-a-nist / noun: a specialist in botany or in a branch of botany: a professional student of plants

Some guy named Phillippe, who is a botanist at one of the major colleges in the big Northeast city near where Corie lives, saw the picture of the pickle-and-fish tree with the two kinds of leaves: one shiny and one not so shiny. He said it was a joke. He said it was impossible. He said, "There is no such tree." He said, "You can't believe every picture you see in the newspaper, even if it is in color." He said he would drive by on Saturday and look at the tree and explain to people how someone made it as a joke and grafted branches from one tree onto another. He said it would take him fifteen seconds to prove it. He said he would then go have lunch at the dog walk/no wife/restaurant guy's place afterwards because he hadn't been there since he was a boy with his father and grandfather back when there were dinosaurs, or at least sauropods.

If you don't know what a sauropod is, kindly ask your librarian to get you a book from the big town nearby. If you live in the big town nearby, then go look on the shelf for it. If it's NOT on the shelf, then perhaps it's one of the five books Corie requested that week.

$1,000,000

Another Thursday.

A lot of Thursdays after the pickle-and-fish tree started growing, the manager of the bank personally came to Corie's house to tell her and her parents and her (somewhat more mature) brothers this:

Even after people in their town, their state, their country, their world, their solar system, their galaxy, and their universe got $773,198.53 cents to buy food, there was still $1,000,000 in the pickle-and-fish tree food charity account.

$3,000,000

Three more Thursdays later, the bank manager came to tell Corie that they had spent $1,909,932.18 on food, and there was $3,000,000 in the account.

That's a lot of money.

And food.

And people being fed.

I forgot what number this is, so I'm going to start using letters.

This is A.

Dad talked to Corie about the fact that there were so many people coming to the yard. He was quite concerned about the money in the donation gurgle bottles that were filling up every day. "It would be a shame if someone stole any money," Dad said.

Corie said not to worry about it and that she would take care of it. "You need money to make money," she reminded him.

Mom and Dad talked about whether she would take care of it or if she was just saying she would take care of it, like she did with the dead plants and the book report and the flossing. Mom thought they should trust Corie, for maybe she WAS growing up.

Corie did take care of it, but you won't know about that until later, and neither will they.

This is B.

On a Saturday and not a Thursday, Phillippe the botanist came to see the pickle-and-fish tree.

He did not have lunch at the dog walk/no wife/restaurant/might-get-married-soon-to-the-lovely-lady-who-likes-dogs-and-goes-for-dog-walks-with-him guy's place. He had lemonade and water and cookies for lunch and dinner and breakfast the next day. He used Corie's phone to call some botanist friends from around the universe.

He used Corie's bathroom after he drank so much lemonade and water with his cookies. Corie was not allowed to charge him a dollar for each bathroom trip. Parents! Who can ever understand them?

His botanist friends, or at least acquaintances, showed up to look at the pickle-and-fish tree. They had lemonade and water and cookies, too, but had to find their own bathrooms.

This is C. (See, Sea)

These things happened, but I don't feel like telling you much about them, so shut off the TV and use your imagination to try and think of what they might have been like:

- Newspapers from around the country and the world showed pictures of the tree/Corie/mud/people/botanist/bank manager.
- TV stations (some who had helicopters and some who wished they had helicopters and even one who had a hot air balloon) from around the country and the world showed pictures of the tree/Corie/mud/people/botanist/bank manager.
- Many donations came in.
- Many people were fed with the donations, and not just at the local grocery store and by the World Food Bank, but by 137 other people-feeding organizations.
- A sign was put up that said, WELCOME TO THE PICKLE-AND-FISH TREE TOWN.
- Corie scored three goals in one soccer game.

- The dog walk/no-wife-yet-but-maybe-a-wife-soon/restaurant guy opened another restaurant in another town. There is a picture of the pickle-and-fish tree on his sign at the new restaurant (which Corie approved, because she owned the trademark, which maybe I will tell you about later because it involved a lot of research and learning), and that restaurant had to open early and stay open late, and there was always a line.
- The police chief in Corie's town had dental work done to replace a cap on a broken tooth.
- Corie and her friends have videotapes and tapes and newspaper clippings and clippings of themselves and each other from all over the world, even the cousins from Canada.
- Much lemonade and water and cookies and sometimes cupcakes and Popsicles were sold.
- Many college fund bank accounts had enough money to send a kid to two colleges or one person to a very expensive college or to a college where instead of a dorm room, they could live in a five-star hotel all year, with leave-it-on-the-floor-because-the-maid-will-get-it service, just from lemonade and cookie sales.

- The sun came up a lot of mornings—that is, umm, it came up every morning, not just a lot of mornings. What I mean is, the sun came up every morning a lot of the time. Oh, you know what I mean.
- It snowed in the Northeast because that's what it does in the Northeast. The weather people on TV got real excited about the snow and drooled and drew lots of charts and graphs about the snow, and sometimes school got cancelled if there was too much snow, even if no small elephants ate the buses.
- Hot chocolate and coffee (yuck!) was sold instead of lemonade and water during those weather person-worried snow times.
- Some botanists rented two houses in town so they could be near the pickle-and-fish tree and look at it every afternoon or morning, and then they had a place to go to the bathroom after they drank lemonade and water—or hot chocolate and coffee—with their cookies.
- The pickle-and-fish tree was properly watered every day, and it grew quite improperly.

I don't like this letters business, so I'm going back to numbers, but I still don't know what number I'm supposed to be on, so I'll start with 47.

Dad was correct.

He often is.

Somebody did try to steal the money in the gurgle jars.

Speaking of money, lots of people from countries around the world came to look at the pickle-and-fish tree and Corie.

When they tried to pay for their lemonade and water or hot chocolate and coffee and cookies, sometimes they didn't have or know how to use American dollars.

Corie did some (but not a lot) of research and determined that they would accept currency, especially coins, from any country in the world. No new sign explaining the pricing in those foreign monies would be posted. If you wanted to pay with your own country money for lemonade or water or hot chocolate or coffee or cookies, then you decided how much you wanted to pay. You got no change because you couldn't use pennies or nickels or dimes or quarters in your country anyway.

Corie and her friends (and their friends and cousins) got to keep all the change and money from foreign countries, and they all have the greatest collections of coins and bills.

When a carload of people put 4,000 yen in for twenty-two cookies, six lemonades, a bunch of Popsicles, and some water, they thought they had enough money to fill up their college savings accounts.

When three busloads of people put half a million lira in for a whole bunch of stuff, they thought they could fill up everybody in town's college savings fund and buy some horses and elephants besides.

Corie did some very thorough research, and there were no horses or elephants or even gerbils bought. Apparently, a lira isn't worth much of anything, not even enough to buy a small gerbil. In fact, in Italy, they don't even use lira anymore. They use Euros. Hmm. Can you imagine that? What if you have a ton of money that you HAD earned from a car wash (that washed even green cars) and all of a sudden one day someone said they were switching the country's money to a Euro or a bureau; I wonder what would happen to all your old money? I guess you could travel around the world and use it to buy lemonade from unsuspecting kids who don't know that it was replaced by bureaus.

One day the bank manager came and asked Corie if he could buy some gildas from the Netherlands from her, but Corie said, "No. They have neat pictures on them."

they got tired of driving around in circles behind the fire truck.

The people on the street—even some kids—and definitely all the dogs woke up, and some of the people—but none of the dogs—walked over to Corie's to see what was going on.

Everyone in Corie's house was kind of going out of their minds, even the policemen/women because the siren was so loud and kept going even after Dad kept turning it off.

Everyone except Corie.

Corie got dressed.

Corie went and found the police chief, who had gotten out of his bed and was in Corie's kitchen. He only lived right down the street anyway.

Corie took her flashlight, and the police chief, and the police chief took his flashlight and two officers (both big ones and "they can walk in front"), and the two officers took their flashlights and followed Corie, who wanted to walk in front but had to walk behind and tell them which way to go and warn them to watch out for the dog poop in the yard that she was supposed to clean up but didn't have time to because of some research she was doing.

Corie took her entourage down to the exact correct, right, perfect, never-been-better, of-course-this-is-the-one-and-only-absolutely-perfect-place-for-it spot where the pickle-and-fish tree was growing with two kinds of leaves, one shiny and one not so shiny.

When they arrived at that spot, there was:

- the world's only (the botanists think) pickle-and-fish tree;
- a hose for watering;
- a small, tasteful sign;
- five gurgle bottles for donations;
- and a man with his hand stuck in one of the gurgle jars.

Eleven minutes later, at that spot, there was:

- the world's only (the botanists think) pickle-and-fish tree;
- a hose for watering;
- a small, tasteful sign;
- five gurgle bottles for donations;
- a man with his hand stuck in one of the gurgle jars;
- the news-picture guy with his camera and lots of film;
- Corie;
- the police chief;
- the two big policemen and most of the other policemen/women and the police dog (lightly dozing);
- Dad;
- Mom;
- Robert;
- James;
- everyone in the neighborhood;

- the no-wife-but-almost/restaurant/pays-the-kids-to-walk-his-dog guy, holding hands with his nice lady;
- three botanists, including one from India;
- no lemonade, water, hot chocolate, coffee, Popsicles, or cookies;
- the ambulance people;
- half the people from the other neighborhoods around there;
- three firemen because they hadn't been called out in a week or two either, and if the ambulance people can drive around at approximately 3:37 in the morning, then they can too;
- no librarians;
- one lady who used to have not much food but gets plenty now, and it's all very nutritious;
- and one very small wire running from the pickle-and-fish tree gurgle donation jars underground in a hole dug with the not-so-new-anymore shovel going all the way up to the house, which is a long way, and in through a window in the basement.

Forty-nine

Corie:

"What's the problem? The police came, and they got the guy, and it was 3:37 in the morning, but it is Saturday, so there's no school anyway."

"Research."

"I know I'm not allowed to do anything with electricity, and I didn't."

"An alarm book."

"It's blue and was published in Denver, Colorado, and our library didn't have a copy, but I'll be happy to donate mine to the library now if it makes you happy."

"What's the problem? The police came, and they got the guy, and it was 3:37 in the morning, but it is Saturday, so there's no school anyway."

"Of course there's a volume setting on the house alarm siren. I have no idea why someone would set it for volume three when it goes all the way up to volume fifteen, and you're always asking me to pick things up, and I did pick up the volume."

"Is what funny?"

"OKAY! Go ahead, switch subjects."

"It takes money to make money."

"A double-looped, spring-activated arm grab in each of the bottles. Why? What's special about that?"

"Well, I thought about doing a triple loop, but I'm quite proud to know that my research and calculations were correct, and a double loop worked just fine."

"All of the money is still there."

"No, I'm not tired, but if you two are, please got to bed right now at eleven a.m., and we can talk later."

"No."

"I think so."

"I could research it if you want."

"I don't understand."

"What's the problem? The police came, and they got the guy, and it was 3:37 in the morning, but it is Saturday, so there's no school anyway."

"Oh, I reprogrammed the alarm. It's quite simple, you know. You just have to move the green-and-white-striped wire from the slot labeled—"

"But you just asked—"

"Well of course there are only seven doors in the house on the alarm, but I wasn't going to hook up the gurgle bottles to the siren using the window wires and not Door Seventy-Three. Do you have any idea how much easier it would have been if I had just used the blue window wire? If something is too easy, you really don't learn as much."

"Yes."

"Under the ground with the new shovel."

"Through the basement window."

"No helpers because it was secret."

"I put it on the alarm, and I'm sure I can take it off."

"Even you can figure out the volume switch...maybe."

"So, you don't want me to donate the blue comes-from-Denver alarm book to the library?"

"I suppose."

"I guess."

"I'm trying."

"Maybe."

"A little harder."

"What's the problem? The police came, and they got the guy, and it was 3:37 in the morning, but it is Saturday, so there's no school anyway."

"Yes, he might have had a gun."

"But I didn't go out there alone. The police went too—even the police chief and he had his picture taken by the news-picture guy."

"The big police guy let me have this police hat. Isn't it great?"

"Yes."

"I suppose."

"3:37 a.m."

"Do you think we'll get more donations?"

"Yes, I can wait until after you get the phone."

Phone.

Phone.

Phone.

Wait.

Phone.

Wait.

Phone.

Wait.

"Yes, I can take the call."

Phone.

Listen...listen...listen...listen...listen...listen...li sten...listen...listen...listen...listen...listen....

"Thanks, Mr. Police Chief, and you're welcome."

Phone done.

"What?

"You want to know EVERYTHING he said?"

"Okay, here goes. That was the police chief. The news-picture guy is going to the police station to take the police chief's picture again with better light in a few minutes. "

"The man with his hand caught in the gurgle jar lives in the next town. He is wanted in Arizona or New Mexico or New Texas or all three for some robberies. They went to his house in the next town, which he lives in half the year when he's not robbing in the Southwest and found stuff that he robs from states in the Northeast in the summer and the spring when the weather is nice."

"In his garage at his house in the next town, they even found a stolen police car. He never has a gun and never steals guns. He likes to steal paintings (and apparently money from gurgle jars). In the bedroom of his house in the next town they found our town's stolen library paper thing."

"That really old important maybe-from-the-Trojan-War-or-at-least-the-Civil-War document that used to be the fourth thing that was in the front of the library before it was stolen that was donated by that really rich old guy who's dead now, but his sister cried and cried when the important war document signed by the President was stolen, and she doesn't want to give any more of her money that she got when her brother died and left it to her to the library to buy books and yogurt, and the head librarian cried when she heard that."

"Yes, that one."

"They found that stolen document in the double-loop-captured-in-the-gurgle-bottle guy's house in the next town."

"I guess he was a real stinker."

These things happened, but I don't feel like telling you much about them, so shut off the TV again (why did you turn it on?) and use your imagination to try and think of what they might have been like:

- The attempted gurgle-stealing guy had a fair trial.
- The attempted gurgle-stealing guy had another fair trial about the other stuff in the Southwest.
- The attempted gurgle-stealing guy had another fair trial about the other, other stuff.
- Some police department I don't know got back their stolen police car, but now it kind of smells funny.
- Jenna got her first-ever goal in a soccer game!
- The police chief had his picture taken by the news-picture guy.
- A wedding invitation came for the whole family from the restaurant/dog walk/soon-to-be-married guy, asking if Corie would be their flower girl or maybe even a bridesmaid if she was too old to be a flower girl.
- Corie's dog (no name) took a nap.

- The police dog lightly dozed.
- The attempted gurgle-stealing guy went to a jail where he couldn't watch cable TV because they don't have it at that jail.
- The botanists used their bathroom a lot because they were up all the time looking at the pickle-and-fish tree and drinking lemonade and water and hot chocolate and coffee (yuck!) and having quite the discussion about stuff that was interesting to botanists but probably no one else.
- It rained.
- The first-ever visitor from the country of Cameroon paid for lemonade and cookies and a lot of Popsicles with some Cameroon money. Do you know what that looks like? You don't? Well, go look it up.
- Extensive research was done on another project. I won't talk about that here, but maybe later I will in another book if you want.
- The police chief had his picture taken again.
- An award was given to Corie and a plaque (not the kind that's on your teeth) was too. "I know it's hung up behind my door and no one will see it there, but then it won't ever get

damaged from people looking at it so much. What?"

- Many donations came in.
- Many people were fed; some of them even got a little chubby.
- A fifth thing was added to the front of the library at the same time that the fourth thing/document/president-signed/war/expensive/stolen/recovered paper was hung back up on the wall with a little green and white wire running from it (and you know where that goes!). The fifth thing that was hung up was a picture of Corie.

Yes.

Corie.

Corie, library trouble-causing, book-requesting, noisy girl.

And the head librarian loved that picture and thought Corie was the best person in the whole world and even gave Corie a key to come in the library anytime she wanted, even if it was closed and it was two in the morning, and if it was closed and it was two in the morning and Corie needed help with any research, she should please call the head librarian at home. "Here's the number, and I will rush right over to the library to help research."

And ALL of the librarians must have taken a class because now you can order any number of books at one time from the other library—not just five—and they can be any size at all, and the rich inherited lady cried and cried when the stolen document was put back up on the wall and she saw the green and white wire (that Corie personally installed and hooked up to the library alarm), and the head librarian actually hugged Corie and had her picture taken with her and keeps that picture on her desk and doesn't eat much yogurt anymore but kind of likes apples much more now, and actually, just last week, I think it was on Thursday, she smiled.

The police chief had his picture taken a lot, but the only time it got in the paper it was on the part of the front page that is below the fold, and you can't really see it when the paper is just kind of lying there, and he did get a medal or something, but Corie's was bigger, and he did get a new flashlight because the other one never really worked right, and he didn't get any stolen police cars back in his department because they never had any police cars stolen in his department, so they had to use their old regular police cars, which do kind of smell funny too.

The police dog is apparently a female police dog because she had nine police dog puppies and doesn't do much police dog work anymore but kind of lives with that family over on the other street and lightly dozes a lot.

The police chief did not smile at all about the picture stuff, even though he had recently been to the dentist for more dental work, including teeth whitening (for pictures).

Oh.

I guess I did want to tell you that library part, and the police chief part.
Anyhoot.

Fifty-One

The botanists finally came out and said that definitely, probably Corie's pickle-and-fish tree was the only pickle-and-fish tree in the whole wide world, and they wanted to name it a Corie Tree, but Corie thought maybe she'd ask if instead they could name it a Phillippe Tree. She did. They did. It was.

Things kind of settled into a routine then, or as routine as things can be when you have (the botanists are almost sure) the only pickle-and-fish tree in the world in your yard. And every single day, your people-feeding charity takes in around a million dollars. And every single day, your feeding-people charity gives away around a million dollars' worth of food. And some important lady from the United Nations wants to give you a medal and put your picture (but not the police chief's picture, even with his whitened teeth) on the cover of your local paper, above the fold.

Oh yeah, I forgot.

Thousands and thousands of people from all over the world now have the local news-picture guy's paper mailed to them every Thursday, or as soon as it can get there by boat and truck and plane and train. The news-picture guy has to talk once a week, more or less, with seventeen miserable, grumpy printer men and women all over the world and tell them how many papers to print. They are all still miserable and grumpy after he hangs up the phone.

Fifty-Two

Routine.

Fifty-Three

Routine.

<u>Fifty-Four</u>

Routine.
Except for the wedding, which was lovely, and Corie was a bridesmaid or maybe a flower girl.

Fifty-Five

Routine.

Fifty-Six

Routine.
But...
...something is starting to happen again
(but nobody knows yet.)

Fifty-Seven: BAM!

It was a Thursday.

It was not raining.

It was early in the morning.

Yelling for help was heard in front of Corie's house.

Corie's whole family, but not the dog, ran out to the pickle-and-fish tree. At the pickle-and-fish tree were the dog walk/restaurant/back-from-the-honeymoon/walking-with-his-new-wife guy and his wife and their dog.

And fifteen fish.

<u>57. BAM! (Some more)</u>

The fifteen fish were:
- flapping on the ground;
- lying in a circle around the pickle-and-fish tree;
- having trouble breathing;
- silver with a little gold, and I think that's purple on top;
- twenty-one inches long;
- not wet at all;
- and being barked at by the dog (not Corie's, the other one).

Corie's family and the restaurant man and his wife:
- ran and got the wheelbarrow;
- ran and got the hose;
- ran and got some buckets;
- filled the wheelbarrow up with water some from the hose and some from buckets filled in the stream;
- ran and got two big trash barrels;
- filled the trash barrels the same way;
- picked up the flapping and flopping fish;
- put four of the fish in the wheelbarrow;
- put six of the fish in one trash barrel;
- put five of the fish in the other trash barrel;

- and stood there looking at the fish with their mouths open and no food in sight, not even the restaurant guy's really, really good rolls with the three kinds of butter that go with them.

f-i-f-t-y—e-i-g-h-t

Helicopters
and vans
and trucks
and police cars
and people
and dogs (on leashes)
and cameras
and TV people
and we ran out of lemonade,
and the ambulance who actually got called
because someone tripped and broke their arm in
two places and broke their toe in one place—the
toe in question had purple nail polish on it—
and sunshine.
and news-picture men and women
and botanists with cellular phones to call fish
study-ers (ichthyologists)
and school busses full of people coming to
look, but they had to park a mile away
and the police chief
and all the librarians because they closed the
library
and nobody from Cameroon, but I think there
were two French ladies with weird shoes
and noise
and open mouths
and shaking heads
and fifteen fish swimming around.

One was swimming very slowly and didn't look so very well.

Are you listening?

I think 1,379,650 people came to see the 15 fish in the first week.

The fish were moved to a huge glass tank that was put right in the middle of Corie's yard because the scientists were afraid to move the fish too far.

Pictures of the fifteen fish were sent all over the world. And research was done all over the world to figure out what kind they were because no one had seen this particular twenty-one inch, silver-with-a-little-gold-and-I-think-that's-purple-on-top fish before.

Or so they thought.

$83,988,014

More than $83,000,000 was donated to the pickle-and-fish tree feeding charity fund in just one week.

Do you know why?

Because everybody hoped the fish wouldn't be used to feed people, so maybe if there was enough money in the pickle-and-fish tree charity account, then the fifteen fish could swim around in the tank in Corie's yard and not have to be used to feed the known universe.

Where did the fish come from?

Shrug!

Sixty-One

Three men and two women had a meeting with the president of Perú.

The president of Perú had his mouth open, and there weren't any rolls to eat in the meeting. He did have a big desk though. He also had quite a nice carpet that had been hand sewn.

Can you imagine how much lemonade, water, hot chocolate, coffee, Popsicles, and cookies 1,379,650 people could eat and drink in one week? Do you have any idea what that would do to a college fund bank account, even if you were from Canada?

Do you have any idea how many people would visit the following week if, on the Thursday after the fifteen fish were found flapping on the ground in a circle around the Phillippe Tree this happened: Fifteen more fish were found! They were scooped up carefully and put in with the other fifteen fish from last Thursday, one of whom was still swimming kind of slowly and did not look so well.

Do you?

Well I don't, but it was a lot.

Chapter Sixty-three

Boys.

Young men.

Young adult males.

One of the quiet conversations Corie's mom and dad had with her a few years ago was about boys and girls and all that.

There was a boy.

He lived in Corie's town. He went to Corie's school. He did not ride on her bus, which was Bus C; he rode on Bus E.

Corie didn't exactly like him.

Really.

Really?

She did kind of sit near-but-not-with him at lunch. He always, always, always, always ate cheese sandwiches for lunch.

Corie didn't always eat the same thing for lunch or sit at the same table, near but not with someone. If she found herself eating the same thing every day or sitting in the same place every day or carrying her backpack the same way every day or wearing the same sneakers every day, well then, she changed.

She even had a cheese sandwich one day and sat with the first graders.

She even had cold leftover meatloaf (with those things in it) and sat in the classroom and worked on her geography thing another day.

Corie has never broken her arm, but she did have stitches in her leg.

Cameroon.

Nothing happened in Cameroon. It's just a neat word: Cameroon. I bet it's a neat place. The people who live there must be Cameroonians or Cameroooners. Do you think they eat cheese sandwiches in Cameroon?

Corie bumped into a tree the first time she went skiing. Also, she bumped into a skinny lady, a kid, two snowboarders, the chair lift, the instructor, Dad, Robert (twice), and a car in the parking lot, which is nowhere near the ski slope. No one knows what she bumped into the second time she went skiing because she hasn't gone again yet. Maybe she will after some research.

Oh!

The library thing.

Corie and the head librarian have lunch together just about every Saturday. The head librarian still gets kind of un-smiley when she thinks of all the kids in town not visiting the library, not even one one-hundredth as much as Corie. She imagines them at home, NOT reading.

So she gets un-smiley.

The head librarian, Corie, Jenna (who's kind of becoming Corie's best friend), the cheese-sandwich-eating boy mentioned above, the third-from-the-head librarian, and some other lady got together.

And they came up with this:

- Corie donated $10,000 from her lemonade money (there's lots more leftover).
- The $10,000 would be hidden in the library.
- The $10,000 would not actually be hidden in the library, and they still have to tell some kids to get out of the offices or basement or duct work and not look there because there really wasn't $10,000 in cash in there.
- The money could be found by figuring out some clues.
- The clues (and clue answers) could be found by reading books.
- Some of the books to read were good-for-you classics books.
- Some of the books to read were not very classic, but fun.
- Some of the books to read were classic and fun
- Some of the books to read were picture books.
- Others of the books to read were chapter books.
- None of the books to read were blue, from-Denver alarm books because the library still didn't have that book.

The reading for clues would take place all summer long. The first person who got the answer on their own would get the money on the first day of school.

The head librarian and the third-from-the-head and the second-from-the-head librarians had a great summer. They met all kinds of new kids. Every day they had a special van go to the big library in the other town to get books, many more than five at a time.

On the first day of school, four kids had the answer. They figured it out on their own and didn't help each other. Two of the kids didn't even like each other at all. One of them had an overbite.

So Corie gave the head librarian $10,000 to give to each of the kids. That makes $40,000 in case you can't add or multiply.

Do you think that is bribing kids to read? Do you? Well it is, and it was, and it did. (But it worked, because some of those kids—but not too, too many—came to the library even after the summer to read more books.)

And every day, the pickle-and-fish tree was watered, and every day it grew, quite improperly.

Corie kind of sat near that boy a couple of times after the first day of school.

Would you like a cheese sandwich?

The president of Perú went on national television.

His mouth was not open, and he was not smiling.

This was what he said:

- There is a fish that is endangered.
- There are less than 1,000 of the fish left in the world.
- The fish can only be found in four small lakes in Perú, one large lake in Perú, and two small lakes in Argentina.
- All five of the lakes in question in Perú are in the sierra, scattered throughout the mountains.
- No aquarium in the world has any of the endangered fish.
- Perú has an Endangered Fish Counting Department.
- Argentina has an Endangered Fish Counting Department.
- Last year, the Endangered Fish Counting Department of Perú counted their endangered fish, and there were seventeen less than the previous year.
- Last year, the Endangered Fish Counting Department of Argentina

counted their endangered fish, and there were three less than the previous year.

- The endangered fish is called a Market (pronounced mar-kay) Fish.
- It has a scientific name something like Ictnatious Alsoaretim Nominite.
- It was named after a famous general that didn't really fight in any wars but limped a lot.
- His name was General Albert Louis Market (pronounced mar-kay).
- The endangered Market (pronounced mar-kay, like the general) Fish is twenty-one inches long.
- The endangered Market (pronounced mar-kay) Fish is silver with a little gold and purple on top
- The thirty fish swimming in the glass tank in Corie's yard near her pickle-and-fish tree are endangered Market (pronounced mar-kay) Fish, and we know because we sent the head counter from the Endangered Fish Counting Department to look.

Other people in the world besides the Perú Endangered Fish Counting Department would not know about Market Fish because Perú does not let anyone take pictures of their Market Fish because they are endangered and shy around cameras and on top of that, they have never even publicly talked or written about their Market Fish before because they are endangered, so that's why the local ichthyologists did not immediately know what kind of fish Corie had.

Perú is talking now.

The president of Perú, and all of the people of Perú, and maybe the president of Argentina (but we haven't checked yet), held Corie personally responsible for whatever happened.

Perú and its president and presumably Argentina's president (but we don't know yet), wanted to know how Corie got thirty endangered Market (pronounced mar-kay) Fish, and they wanted to know right away.

Well...

Things sure are happening, aren't they?

The local ichthyologists decided to sleep in front of the tank so they could be near the Market (in case you don't know by now, it's pronounced mar-kay) Fish and maybe not let any counters from Perú take them.

The police chief decided to park a police car in Corie's driveway and have two policemen/women sit there all day and night and not doze at all.

Mom and Dad decided to have lots of quiet conversations late at night and worry.

The botanists decided to sleep in front of the pickle-and-fish tree, and if they drank too much lemonade or water or hot chocolate or coffee, they could walk home to their rented house's bathroom.

Mom decided that Dad would NOT call the president of Perú and say, "If you hadn't taken all of your Market (pronounced mar-kay) Fish to the market (pronounced FOOD Mark-it) and eaten them, they wouldn't be endangered."

The news-picture guy decided to print a big map of Perú in his paper showing the coastal plain, the sierra, and the montaña, with little stars where all the Market Fish lakes are.

The president of Perú decided to call the president of the United States for a discussion, maybe with some back-and-forth, and maybe with only some forth.

The restaurant/dog walk/married guy decided that the nightly specials would be:

- Sonoma Goat Cheese Ravioli with Shitake Mushrooms, Basil, and Sundried Tomatoes;
- Rotisserie Lamb Chops in a Mediterranean Salad with Brick Oven Naan, Pancetta-Fig Satay Melted Eggplant, and Pomegranate Vinaigrette;
- and Peanut Butter and Jelly Sandwiches on Plain White Bread.

The head counters for the Endangered Fish Counting Departments of both Perú and Argentina decided to do a new special count of their Market Fish (I think you know how it's pronounced by now!)

Some television people and some scientists decided to set up a bunch of cameras all around the pickle-and-fish tree before next Thursday to see if any more fish showed up.

And Corie?

Corie played soccer and fed Jenna an absolutely perfect pass right in front of the goal, and Jenna got her second goal of the season!

And Corie watered her pickle-and-fish tree properly every day, and...well, by now you know how it grew.

Well, it's hard to believe we're up to sixty-six. If you're interested, sixty-six is all about some jobs.

There was a lot of money going into the pickle-and-fish tree charity account. There was a lot of money being spent by the pickle-and-fish tree charity group.

A group? Yes, a group.

The pickle-and-fish tree charity had an official Board of Directors, the people who decide what gets done with all the money. Yes, I know I said Corie gets to decide everything, but that was a while ago. Now there's so much money and so much feeding that a group of people works together to decide.

The Board of Directors of the pickle-and-fish tree charity fund included:

- Corie,
- Corie's dad,
- the bank manager,
- the restaurant/dog walk guy's wife,
- a lady who used to work for the World Food bank in Geneva,
- two guys you don't know named Forrest Schroth and Mark Silva,
- the news-picture owner,
- the head librarian (she's really, really nice),

- and Corie's brother, James, who's becoming quite mature.

There is an awful lot of work to do. There is change from the gurgle jars to count and deposit at the bank. There is mail to open. There are checks to process. There are bank statements to read and figure out. There are people-feeding organizations from around the world that need to be researched—every day and every week.

Someone came up with a great idea. You know all those people whose name is on the list at the grocery store? The people who don't have enough money for food? Well, the reason some of them don't have enough money for food is because they don't have jobs.

The pickle-and-fish tree charity group needed help, and some people needed jobs. Put the two together, and you get jobs for people right in town! "And if you have a baby that you're taking care of and that's why you can't work, bring the baby, and we'll set up daycare for you."

Do you know who came up with that idea?

It was Corie's brother James. He's getting quite mature and hasn't bopped anyone on the arm in a while.

Anyhow. Anyhoom. Anymature.

Oh! That Mister Schroth from the Board of Directors of the Charity Feeding Group has a very nice daughter named Alexis. If you ever meet her, tell her I said hello.

My favorite number is 67.

Are you an adult?

If you're not, then have you ever seen a dandelion?

Do you know what it is?

Did you ever hear your parents talk about them?

In case you don't know (and you probably don't because you've never seen one), it's a weed. It's a pretty weed with nice, big, yellow flowers on it.

Are you an adult?

If you are, then…

Do you remember when you were a kid?

Do you remember all the dandelions in people's yards?

Do you know that it's a weed?

Do you know that it has pretty yellow flowers?

You do? You remember that?

Good. Then explain this please:

Why do you adults go out of your way to kill off all the dandelions?

Don't you want kids to see them? Did the dandelions do something to you when you were kids? Did they bite? Did they trip you when you were playing soccer and received a great pass right in front of the goal and didn't score because you fell? Were they poisonous? Did your parents make you eat them for dinner? For dessert? Did you have to do extra homework on weekends about them?

Why do you have trucks come by your house and spray some junk on your yards so there will be no dandelions?

Don't you want kids to see them?

And who came up with the junk to spray on your lawns? Was it some weird dandelion-killing scientist who hates dandelions even more than you and doesn't want his kids to see them? And instead of thinking about killing dandelions, why wasn't that scientist thinking about how to feed more people?

Do-be-do. Anyhoo.

The next Thursday, fifteen more fish were found around the tree and carefully helped into the tank.

Everybody keeps looking at the TV tapes over and over, but no one can figure out what happened. One second there were no fish. The next second, fifteen flopping, flapping, having-trouble-breathing, silver-with-a-little-gold-and-I-think-that's-purple-on-top fish were around the tree.

And it happened the following Thursday too.

But then it stopped.

One tank.

Gobs and gobs of charity money.

And that one fish is swimming normally now.

Anyhow.

No number or letter. In fact, not really a chapter. Just some facts. Think of it kind of like research.

Perú:

- is divided into three main topographical areas: the coastal plain, the sierra, and the montaña (I don't know what that squiggle thing is over the n, but I like it);
- is the third largest country in South America; (Guess which is biggest. Go on...guess. Nope. Guess again. Brazil? Right! Now, guess which is second biggest. Nope, try again. Argentina? Right!);
- is 496,225 square miles (that's 1,285,216 square meters);
- has that montaña part, which is a vast tropical plain that stretches all the way to Brazil and is actually part of the Amazon basin (You know what the Amazon is, don't you? No, I don't mean that Internet place where you can buy books. It's a river.);
- has weather;
- had a population in 1989 (a very good year) of 21,256,731;

- had a population in 2011 (a very strange grapefruit year for me) of 29,248,943;
- has a capital called Lima;
- has people that speak mostly Spanish but also Quechua;
- has a national library in Lima that has more than 3.2 million books and other things;
- uses Nuevos Soles for money;
- and has a canyon named the Colca Canyon, which is two times as deep as the Grand Canyon in the U.S. AND is the deepest canyon on Earth.

The president of Perú had an announcement to make.

It was very important, and everyone should have listened and watched.

The head counters for the Endangered Fish Counting Departments of both Perú and Argentina finished their new special count of their Market (pronounced mar-kay, in case you forgot) Fish. I think they might have been trying to find which particular lake Corie's Market Fish came from.

They Endangered Fish Counting Department found their last year's report and dusted it off, and this is what that somewhat dusty old report said.

Perú Little Lake #1 had 147 Market Fish last time we counted.

Perú Little Lake #2 had 58 Market Fish last time we counted.

Perú Little Lake #3 had 101 Market Fish last time we counted.

Perú Little Lake #4 had 30 Market Fish last time we counted.

Perú Big Lake #1 had 529 Market Fish last time we counted.

Argentina Little Lake #1 had 73 Market Fish last time we counted.

Argentina Little Lake #2 had 49 Market Fish last time we counted.

The Endangered Fish Counting Department must also have an Adding Up Department because they did add up those numbers and reported that the not-so-grand total of all of those endangered fish last year was 987.

That's not a lot of fish for so many little and big lakes, even if they are in Perú and Argentina.

The Endangered Fish Counting Department talked about their new special count that was requested by the president with the hand-sewn rug. Here is what they found:

Perú Little Lake #1 has 2350 Market Fish now.

Perú Little Lake #2 has 3109 Market Fish now.

Perú Little Lake #3 has 3576 Market Fish now.

Perú Little Lake #4 has 1003 Market Fish now, including three that swim rather slowly and don't look so good.

Perú Big Lake #1 has 12,899 Market Fish now.

Argentina Little Lake #1 has 4,066 Market Fish now.

Argentina Little Lake #2 has 3,454 Market Fish now.

The Endangered Fish Adding Up Department must have had to work a lot of weekends and nights because those are kind of biggish numbers and could take a bit of time to add up, even if you had one of those fancy calculators with the roll of paper that spit out the top. Do you have any idea how long those rolls are if you stretch them all the way across your front yard? Well, Corie doesn't know either. The one time she tried stretching the calculator roll all across the front yard she was stopped before she even made if off the walkway.

Anycount!

When they did spend all that time adding up those numbers, I hope someone thought to bring them something to eat. Perhaps a cheese sandwich or two.

And some pudding.

Counting done, adding done, and the QUITE GRAND total? 30,457 Market (pronounced WOW that's a lot of mar-kay) Fish.

Check my math if you want.

You know what else they said?

They found Market Fish (pronounce it any way you want) in ten more lakes in Perú and five more lakes in Argentina and even three lakes in Chile, and Chile doesn't even have an Endangered Fish Counting Department, but they're going to start one.

There were so many fish in those new lakes they hadn't even had time to count them yet!

S-e-v-e-n-t-y. We're getting close to the end.

One week, the specials at the dog walk/happily married guy's restaurant were:

- Grilled Pork Tenderloin with Polenta and Balsamic Smothered Cremini Mushrooms;
- Warm Artichoke Salad with Hobb's Proscuitto and Handmade Parmesan Breadstick;
- Spit-Fired Chicken with Pan-Roasted Herb Dumplings and Mustard Seed Broth;
- Udon Noodle Bowl with Exotic Mushrooms, Glazed Tofu, and Miso Boullion;
- and Two Peanut Butter, Jelly, and M&M Sandwiches Shaped Like Elephants with Double Potato Chips.

And no Market Fish...not ever.

Well, well, Wellington, New Zealand!

I wonder if that is near Old Zealand. I also wonder if that is anywhere near New AaaLand or Old AaaLand.

What was happening in New Zealand? I have no idea. All I know is what was happened around Corie's land. This:

- A big water pipe broke on Main Street, not near the library but sort of near the bank.
- Corie's braces got taken off.
- Jenna's braces got adjusted again, and she chose pink and blue bands.
- The restaurant//dog/wife guy's other restaurant had a small kitchen fire, but no one was hurt, and damage was minimal.
- One of the women who used to not have enough food (her name was on the grocery list, but then she worked at Corie's charity doing bookkeeping and mailing checks, and her name isn't on the list anymore) is running for senator of Corie's state, and she might actually win.
- Geneva, Switzerland wanted to put up a small, tastefully done statue of Corie

kind of near the edge of Lake Geneva, but Corie asked them to please not to, so they put up a statue of the pickle-and-fish tree instead and a small, tastefully done sign. Phillippe visited it while he was over in Paris and took a train down to Geneva, which isn't a bad train ride if you ever have the time, and you can even eat yogurt on the train if you want. They might even let you yodel since it sounds almost like yogurt. Research that before you go please.

- The head librarian had an operation on a pinched nerve in her back, and she feels much better now.
- The police chief did not even have his picture taken for six whole weeks.
- The sixty Market Fish were moved from Corie's front yard to the aquarium in the big city, but they won't be there long because they're going to Perú or Argentina or Chile to a lake to maybe to meet some other Market Fish and settle down and have Market Fish babies.
- Corie often went all by herself and sat with her back against her pickle-and-fish tree and just kind of thought about stuff or read or lightly dozed. She liked sitting there, and I think the tree liked it too.

The president of Perú does not tell lies.

Never, not ever. Not even once. Not even those little sort-of white lies or kind-of-not-really-answering-the-question-but-not-quite-a-lie lies.

He tells the truth.

Always.

Do you remember from a while ago how the president of Perú said he would hold Corie personally responsible for whatever happened? Do you? It wasn't that long ago. Do you remember?

Well good if you do, and have your memory checked if you don't.

The president of Perú did hold Corie personally responsible.

Here's what the President of Perú held Corie responsible for:

- for growing a pickle-and-fish tree in her yard;
- for the sixty Market Fish that would be coming from the aquarium to meet other Market Fish in a Perú lake;
- and for the fact that there are now more than 50,000 Market Fish all over lots of South America, so many they can't even count them all, even with all

their Endangered Fish Counting Departments.

The President of Perú does not tell lies

Here's what the President of Perú said (truthfully). Corie was a saint. Corie was the most wonderful child in the world. God himself sent Corie down from heaven to save the Market Fish and grow pickle-and-fish trees.

He would fly to America and meet Corie and thank her for all the Market (pronounced mar-kay) Fish. He would like Corie to come to Perú, and she would be a national hero and they would have parades for her or fireworks if she wants

and they would name a park or a hospital or a street or even a city or a lake after her

and if she does come to Perú, she can stay anywhere she likes

and go to the bathroom anywhere she likes

and won't be charged one dollar or even 1 New Sol

and she can even stay in the president's house

and not just the president's kind of smallish forty-five-room house in Lima, the capital, but his big house near Trujillo in the north of Perú near the ocean with the beach and the helicopter and its own private lake and lawn chairs.

The President of Perú does not tell lies

Here's what the President of Perú did.

He went to Corie's town and met Corie.

He had lemonade and water and cookies and paid for it with some really cool Perúvian coins called Nuevos Soles, some with pictures of generals on them.

He went to dinner with Corie and her family at the restaurant/dog walk/happily married guy's place.

He had the rolls with the three kinds of butter and loved them.

He drove around Corie's town in the police chief's new car.

Did I forget to tell you about the police chief's new car?

Oh! I did.

Corie felt really bad about the police chief always getting his picture taken and never getting it on the cover, especially not above the fold, so Corie used some of her lemonade money (there's still tons left) and bought him a new police car that doesn't smell and has his name written on the side.

The police chief was happy for a whole day! He was happy until the next day, which was a Thursday, and the local paper came out and his picture wasn't on the cover, but instead there was a picture of his new police car with his name on it.

Above the fold.

The Perú President also:

- visited the aquarium and saw the sixty Market Fish, who were getting on a plane that very afternoon (who knew fish could fly?);
- liked Corie's dog and petted her a lot;
- told the truth the whole time he visited;
- met the woman who is now a senator of Corie's state;
- used the not-very-new-anymore shovel to dig a hole and plant a Perúvian tree he had brought with him right in Corie's yard, kind of down by the stream;
- and sat outside late at night when no one was around next to Corie with his back resting on the Phillippe Tree and thought and lightly dozed.

Corie went to the movies with that young adult male I mentioned earlier, while her dad saw the movie in the next theater, but it wasn't really a "date."

No cheese sandwiches were consumed.

73 The Pickle-and-Fish Tree

I haven't really told you much about the Phillippe Tree lately.

Here are the facts:

- It is properly watered every day.
- It is exactly 787.5 inches tall.
- It is exactly 65 feet, 7.5 inches tall.
- It is exactly, exactly, exactly 20 meters tall. (Isn't that odd?)
- It doesn't grow any taller but stays exactly the same height.
- It has a trunk part that is exactly 5 meters tall.
- It has a big leafy part that is exactly 15 meters tall.
- It looks like a big, perfectly round, light green and dark green 15-meter round beach ball.
- It still has the two kinds of leaves, one shiny and one not so shiny.
- In the fall, some of the leaves turn colors and fall off, but not all of them.
- The leaves that don't fall off stay green (light or dark) all winter long.
- The colors the leaves that fall off turn are peach, pink, and light yellow.

Anyone can take a leaf that falls off, and they don't even have to donate money into the gurgle jars (but they always do).

<u>More and More in Seventy-Four</u>

The botanists, led by Phillippe, went on national television. They had an announcement to make, something important about pickle-and-fish trees. The botanists announced that they were now wrong. There were more pickle-and-fish trees in the world!

Are you a little excited by that? Are you glad there are more pickle-and-fish trees? Are you wondering how improperly they will grow? Are you a little disappointed by that? Did you kind of want Corie (or yourself) to be the only one in the world with a pickle-and-fish tree?

Well, don't be disappointed! That's goofy!

The botanists found pickle-and-fish trees growing:

- near the stream by Corie's front yard (three of them!);
- in Corie's side yard;
- in Corie's back yard;
- diagonally across the street at Jenna's house;
- down the street at the police chief's house;
- in the yard of that big blue house behind the fire station;
- and one in St. Louis, Missouri, down by the Mississippi River, kind of near

where all those riverboats are, growing through a crack in the cement.

Chapter 75

On November 17, the president (not of Perú, but of the United States of America, as in White House, Washington D.C., etc.) is going to visit the big Northeast city near where Corie lives. He's also going to visit Corie's town. He is going to go and see Corie's Phillippe Tree and maybe give her a thanks-for-feeding-all-the-people-in-the-universe medal and have some lemonade, and he gets to go to the bathroom in the house for free too.

And if you figure out where the president (U.S., not Perú) is on November 17, then you'll know the name of that big Northeast city, and you'll probably be able to figure out Corie's town, which is kind of a little north of there. It should be pretty easy, because there's a big sign that says:

WELCOME TO THE HOME OF THE
PICKLE-AND-FISH TREE

But I'm still not going to tell you the name of Corie's dog, because you might steal the dog.

Corie's brother's names are still Robert and James though.

SeVeNtY SiX

Corie (to Mom and Dad):
"Sure, I have time to talk."
"Yes."
"Okay."
"Thank you."
"Yes, it's been great."
"I know."
"I guess I did."
"Oh! She's great. I'm glad she's the head librarian. This summer, she and Jenna and a few others and I (and maybe even him), are going to do another reading thing, and this time we're inviting people from all over the state, and there are some huge surprises, and we think even more people will get excited about reading."
"Yes, that's true."
"Mature?"
"Really?"
"Responsible? Following through? Growing up? ME?"
"You think so?"
"I guess I never noticed it."
"Well, yes! I'm glad people are being fed, even in countries not on the maps yet, and there's money to feed them and give them jobs, and nobody has to eat the Market Fish, and I think James does a great job running the charity and being mature and going to college too."

"Me?"

"I guess I was responsible, but so many friends and people from all over helped."

"It is wonderful."

"Yes."

"I wish the police chief would smile more, and after the reading thing at the library in the summer, I'm going to work on that."

"Thank you."

"Wow."

"That's really nice of you to say."

"Not quite the whole universe!"

"Yes."

SeVeNtY-SeVeN

Corie: Tall, thin, scruffy, female, student, blondish, smart, creative, outspoken, trouble-finding, precocious (whatever THAT means), eager, mature, silly, immature, messy-roomed, imaginative, animal-loving, universe-feeding girl.

Colon: B

78 Finish?

You know the pickle-and-fish tree?

The tree that's perfectly round, shaped like a big light green and dark green beach ball? The one that never grows any taller but stays exactly the same height?

Well, there's a new very, very, very, very skinny branch starting to grow very, very quickly right out of the exact top of it, and it's already about three feet tall.

Nobody has seen it yet.

Except Corie.

She noticed it last Thursday.

milk milk

Banal4

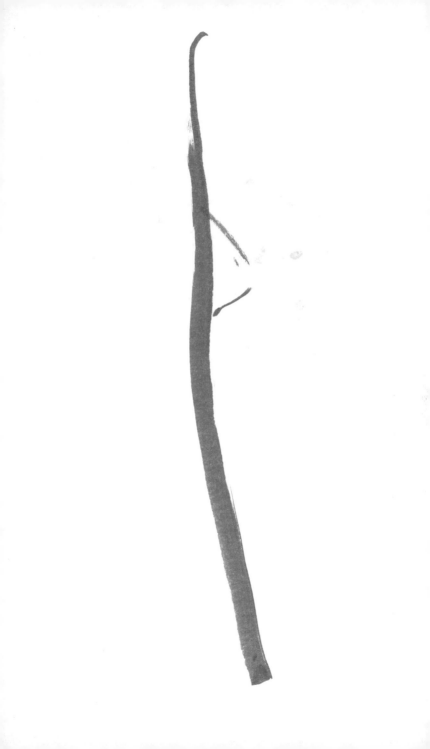

Made in the USA
Lexington, KY
27 December 2012